CW00506354

Days and Nights in W12

Jack Robinson is a freelance writer and editor living in West London. He has also published *Recessional* (CBe, 2009), a collage of text and photographs, rant and reflection, written during the early months of the recession.

'What Robinson does is create a kind of twilight zone of west London, doing for Shepherd's Bush what J. G. Ballard did for Shepperton ... As well as recurring themes, stories and people cross-refer throughout the book, though Robinson's voice is what really gives the book unity. His sense of absurdity mixed with social awareness is habit-forming.' – John Self, *Asylum*

Days and Nights in W12

Jack Robinson

CB *editions*

'I was never without a piece of soap, whenever I happened to be knocking about the Shepherd's Bush area.'

– Davies, in Harold Pinter, *The Caretaker*

This edition first published in 2011
by CB editions
146 Percy Road London W12 9QL
www.cbeditions.com

Some of this material was included
in a previous edition published in 2007.

All rights reserved

© Jack Robinson, 2007, 2011

The right of Jack Robinson to be identified
as author of this work has been asserted in accordance
with the Copyright, Designs and Patents Act, 1988

Printed in England by ImprintDigital, Exeter EX5 5HY

ISBN 978–0–9561073–7–4

ABC

Midnight. A stranger is at the door. She tells you she needs money for the bus fare down to Exeter, where her father is dying of liver cancer, and she hasn't seen him for six years and the fare is £25.50 and the bus leaves at 3.30 a.m. and earlier today she was mugged in the park, and you know that if you don't interrupt her all the awful details are just going to go on piling up. Do you give her the benefit of the doubt? Equally, when you press the buzzer yourself and a voice through the intercom – the voice of someone who has been interrupted in an afternoon nap or a game of chess or an argument about who puts out the rubbish or an idyllic bout of love-making – tells you the person you want has gone away and maybe you'd best do that same thing yourself: to believe or not to believe? Do you need evidence before you decide? For some of these stories – for example, those of Sri Aurobindo (page 9) or Juliet Herbert (page 42) – I can quote chapter and verse from other sources; for others, there's only what's here in black and white.

A&E

The waiting time in A&E this afternoon is three hours and thirty minutes. And truly, no one here looks as if they are about to die *right now*, or even in the next half hour; it feels more as if their flight has been delayed. When you look more closely you see that that woman's head is tilted at a strange angle, and that man's left ankle seems swollen, much bigger than his other one, but none of us is perfect and these flaws could simply be part of who they are, although of course God knows what's going on beneath the surface. Every twenty minutes or so a nurse comes to the edge of the room and calls out a name, giving it an upward inflection at the end, unsure of her pronunciation, unsure such a person even exists. A child mewls. The drinking fountain is out of order. A silent TV screen shows a continuous loop of advice – drink responsibly, recycle, save water – though it may be too late for all that now. After around an hour you are learning how to wait, and beginning to accept that hurt, pain, error and the need for help are not accidents or emergencies at all.

ALLOTMENT

A woman lives in this allotment shed. She mixes her tobacco with the dried leaves of a plant she grows here, and she drinks vodka in which the leaves of some other plant have been infused. She wears many layers of clothes and the colour of her eyes changes: green when she laughs, red when she's angry, yellow when sad, a kind of deep purple when her memory is playing tricks. So many different colours and shades. She has friends who sit with her and talk, and sometimes in winter, when the allotments are untended and there may be snow on the ground, I take a vodka contribution and join them. Often I end up staying the whole night: when her eyes are blue or green the hours pass quickly, and no one wants to leave her alone when they're yellow.

APE

The DNA of this ape is 99 per cent identical with my own. He follows me, or I him; I glance into a shop window and he's there. Sometimes he opens his great foul-smelling mouth and cries out, 'a cry that was no more than a breath'. Mistah Kurtz – he not dead yet.

AUSTIN A35

Given that losing and forgetting are most of what we do, the appearance of this Austin A35 in a multi-storey car park like a dollop of thick grey custard is an act of comic revenge. In the 1950s we – my mother, my brother, myself – were encapsulated in this car for many thousands of miles (it's roughly the same size as Vostok 1, in which Yuri Gagarin orbited the Earth in 1961); at picturesque spots or for family reunions we stepped out and took black-and-white photos of each other with our Kodak Brownie camera. I open the unlocked door and sit behind the wheel but the wind has been through it – there is nothing, not even a whiff of those journeys: the boredom, bickering, silences, the close-quarters intensity of other people's moods, the desperate holding on until we can stop to pee by the roadside. Just some hairs on the back seat that may be dog hairs. Children grow up in such boxed, cramped spaces, between one place and another.

BAKERY

It was raining and David's wife asked if he could give her a lift down to the Tube station. He was busy, he was looking at job ads for marketing managers on the computer, but he checked the time and said yes, and he drove her to the Tube station and on the way back he parked in a side street and popped into the baker's, because at around four o'clock they sometimes sell off the day's bread cheap. And now he's been walking for over an hour, looking for his car; he is discovering streets he didn't know existed, even though they're so local, and is soaking wet and his life is unravelling. A traffic warden will have got there first and the trip will have cost him £60. All his minor resentments of his wife – the way she never closes cupboard doors, the way she asks what time it is even though he told her five minutes ago, her spelling mistakes, her *shoes*, and why couldn't she have taken the bus? – are building to a head: they should never have got married, divorce is now the only honest option. At his age, no one will employ him in marketing ever again. It becomes clear that he must immediately return to the baker's shop and ask for a job – never mind the early rising and the low pay, people will always need bread and if he's got nowhere to live he can even sleep there, next to the ovens at the back where it's warm and dry.

BIRD OVER PRISON WALL

To escape – as the convicted spy George Blake did from this prison in 1966, using a rope ladder whose rungs were made of knitting needles – you need courage, self-belief and meticulous planning and attention to detail, besides contempt for the regime you are living under. (These qualities are possibly much the same as those that got you into the place you're now trying to get out of.) Then there is luck – a guard momentarily distracted, a pile of sand that cushions your fall after you miss a foothold – which you cannot determine, but which sometimes you can feel in your bones, as light as air, as in the hollow bones of birds that enable them to fly.

BLOCK OF FLATS

On the fourth floor of this building is the present location of what the police refer to as 'The VIP Lounge'. (By the time you read this, it will have moved on.) It is a diversion on the route from the centre of town to Heathrow airport. For a generous fee, cab drivers will bring passengers with expensive luggage to the VIP Lounge to meet with four brothers – who have been variously described by the disoriented passengers as black, white, Arab, tall, swarthy, 'of medium build', etc. In a parody of a customs examination at the airport, the brothers will meticulously unpack the luggage and discuss with its owners their clothing, souvenirs, foreign currency, cameras, laptops, sex toys, whatever. Then, after confiscating certain items of value, the brothers will wish bon voyage to the passengers, who are driven blindfold to another part of town, from where they must hurry to catch their planes. This personalised form of robbery, involving relaxed communication between thief and victim, represents a sophisticated new trend in contemporary crime.

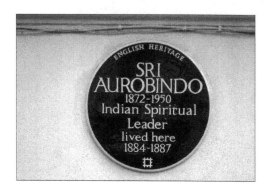

BLUE PLAQUE

Sri Aurobindo lived in this house in St Stephen's Avenue during his early teens, before going to Cambridge to read the Classics and prepare for the Indian Civil Service examinations. (He passed the academic exams with distinction, then decided he didn't want to be an administrator and failed to turn up for the obligatory horse-riding test.) He later became a political activist in India, was imprisoned for his suspected involvement in the attempted assassination of a British official, and developed an influential philosophy of spiritual evolution. His father didn't live to witness this part of Aurobindo's life, nor read even one of the 24,000 lines of Aurobindo's spiritual epic in blank verse which recounts the victory of humanity over ignorance, suffering and death: he died heartbroken after being misinformed that his son, on his return voyage to India in 1893, had died in a shipwreck off the coast of Portugal.

BOAT UNDER WRAP

W12 is landlocked. But when a tidal wave sweeps over the Thames Barrier and when the floodwaters from the river rise above the 10-metre contour line, much of Shepherd's Bush will be under water. In back gardens, in yards and garages, there are boats kept in readiness. Once or twice a year their owners, led by the Admiral, take the boats down to the river for training exercises. The boat-people believe themselves to be rational and far-sighted; to outsiders they appear more like a millennial cult who can barely wait for the Day of Judgement to arrive, and security staff at the Thames Barrier are on high alert for acts of sabotage.

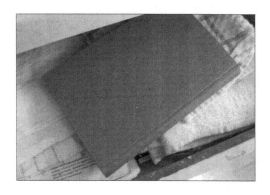

BOOK IN A DRAWER

This book, by a famous Hungarian author, is kept in a drawer not because it is pornographic but because it belongs to a man who used to come two or three times a week to the Café Gama for coffee in the afternoons. On the days when he forgot the book, or couldn't find it, he was anxious and restless, and often left before he'd finished his coffee. Cem (pronounced, probably incorrectly, Jam), who runs the café, suggested that he leave the book in a drawer behind the serving counter, so that he'd always know where it was. The man read very slowly: after a period of some four months, from February to May, his bookmark – an envelope with an illegible address – was still around twenty pages from the end. It's September now, and the man hasn't been back. Cem thinks he must feel frustrated, not to know the end of the story, how everything turns out. He'd like to know himself, but he can't read Hungarian.

BRICKFIELD

After a demolition (here, of a swimming pool), the land takes on the appearance of 'the broken borders of the brickfields, smelling of the clay from which they had swollen', as described by Arthur Machen (see page 51) in Shepherd's Bush in the 1890s. In Machen's *Hill of Dreams*, they inspire an hallucinatory disgust: 'Nothing fine, nothing rare, nothing exquisite, it seemed, could exist in the weltering suburban sea, in the habitations which had risen from the stench and slime of the brickfields. It was as if the sickening fumes that steamed from the burning bricks had been sublimed into the shape of houses, and those who lived in these grey places could also claim kinship with the putrid mud.' For me they are the hour of the wolf, that unclaimed, interim time between night and dawn or, on a cold winter afternoon, between the dying of daylight and the coming of darkness, when no one seems to know whether to switch on the lights yet or wait a bit longer.

BUSKERS IN THE TUBE

They sing the old songs, the songs of the time before we became commuters and married and mortgaged up to the hilt, before we became who we are. The lyrics haunt us, we know them by heart, so never mind that they are playing on this and we are a soft touch, and never mind that they made the corporate lawyers rich and fat and that permission to quote them in print would cost the earth. When the hat comes round, be generous.

CAFÉ TABLE

Anna's husband has left her, after twenty years of marriage. She seems to be coping well, in fact is more sociable and optimistic than I've known her for years. But she still goes every Sunday morning to the same café she and her husband used to frequent, and is served by the same waiter, to whom the word surly doesn't begin to do justice. He is maybe sixty years old, and smells sour. He never smiles, he rarely speaks, he makes her wait; the coffee is cold when he brings it, and spills onto the saucer when he slams it down on the table. He is the patron saint of stubborn gloom. Occasionally the café takes on a part-time waitress, the kind who is cheerful and wants to practise her English, but only the grumpy waiter is allowed to serve Anna and these girls soon move on. I've suggested to Anna that she take her custom elsewhere, but she won't hear of it. They are locked together, Anna and this waiter, in a grim contest of fidelity.

CARROT-WOMAN

With her strawberry sister lurking nearby, the woman dressed as a carrot represents, I suppose, a new juice bar. But it's rash to suppose anything as innocent as that. She may believe that she *is* a carrot; far from the fertile plains, she is crying for help.★ Shoppers hurry by, not meeting her eyes. We are a nation of shoppers now, not shopkeepers: eager but watchful, wary of being deceived by the difference between what things are and what they claim to be. Here in the mall actors are working as wine-bar waiters, philosophy professors as cleaners, terrorists as security guards.

★ The only reason, Empson said, that Coleridge was not a vegetarian was that he believed carrots have feelings too. Turner and his patron Lord Egremont, according to Thornbury's *Life* (1862), once had an argument about whether carrots can float, an argument resolved only when 'Lord Egremont rings the bell, and calls for a bucket of water and some carrots'.

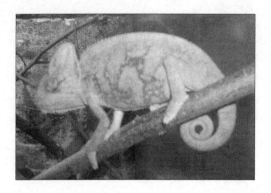

CHAMELEON

This chameleon is in a shop that also sells rabbits, parrots, canaries and budgies, pigeons, rats, toads, tropical fish, a solitary flesh-eating piranha and sometimes kittens. If you are thinking of buying a pet here, there is man with a shaven head further down the market who will be able to tell you its pedigree. This parrot was, in its previous life, a royal princess; this canary was a worm; this rat, a traffic warden. In the cycle of reincarnation, living beings may ascend to higher level or go down. The attitude of the pet-shop owner to the shaven-headed man is also changeable, because sometimes the man can persuade potential purchasers to buy, and at an inflated price, and sometimes he puts them off. At bottom, the pet-shop owner distrusts the shaven-headed man: we have one life, he believes, and when it's over that's it, and anything else is mumbo-jumbo. The shaven-headed man says that in his previous life the pet-shop owner was a world-famous film actor, but he will not say what sins he committed to arrive at where he now is.

CHILDREN STOPPED BY POLICE

The little people are being searched by the big people (it's usually this way round). What the police are looking for is knives or drugs; what they are finding, I hope, is chewing gum and marbles. But whatever comes out of the children's pockets (and by the law of averages, one of those pockets is bound to contain something incriminating), and despite the fact that they are bunking off school, they are learning a lesson: not to be in the wrong place at the wrong time. Exactly where the right place might be and when is still unclear.

CHIMNEYS

Nothing moves. Grey sky, no wind, a dead afternoon in the suburbs with no news from the frontier and the bass on my neighbour's music turned up slightly too high. I think of the long afternoons of childhood, and far back beyond those to the Period of the Three Kings,★ a time so remote even their names are smoke.

★ Each of whom had three daughters. Or one daughter with three suitors. Always the hero has to pass three tests. Always three underground chambers, three bells and cats and ships. Three dishes, three wishes, three knocks on the door.

From birth a gifted spiritual healer, love and relationship specialist. I can Succeed where other people have failed.

PROBLEMS CONCERNING:

Love, marriage, bad luck, black magic, business, Immigration, court cases, sexual impotency, exams, and careers etc.

NO DISAPPOINTMENT

Very rapid result 100% guaranteed. Speaks also French and Spanish.

For appointment call·

CLAIRVOYANT

Madame Sosostris, famous clairvoyante, had a bad cold. Nevertheless I kept my appointment, needing help with certain problems (not all of the above, but among them); needing, in a word, to be saved. She was younger than I'd expected, a thin, angular woman wrapped in shawls with knotted fringes; her breath wheezed as she spoke; the air in the tiny room was close, almost sticky, as sticky as the much-thumbed cards she laid out on the table. A damp tissue was tucked inside her tasselled sleeve. If she could see so clearly, I thought, why couldn't she save herself? Why couldn't I learn to trust myself, rather than her? I knew already, for example, before she had turned the cards, that one was the Fool and another the Hanged Man. I knew I would be sneezing by the time I got home, and would have to buy a pack of Lemsip on the way.

CLASSROOM

The thirteen students in the life class include housewives, account-
ants, a bus driver and a retired policeman. The atmosphere is relaxed;
all are perfectly at ease with the naked model, focusing conscien-
tiously on their eye-to-hand coordination and the figure-ground re-
lationships. The boy next to Megan, the youngest in the class, works
quickly and with an amazing facility – surely, she thinks, comparing
his fluent drawing with her own tentative, inhibited lines, he has no
need to be in this class at all. Suddenly he rips his drawing from its
board and tears it up. She looks at him, puzzled. He speaks with a bad
stammer: 'It's b-b-b-bad – I can n-n-n-never . . .' She looks away, as
from the revelation of something intimate.

CLOUD

'Methinks it is like a weasel.' – 'It is backed like a weasel.' – 'Or like a whale?' – 'Very like a whale.' From the window of her tiny room above a betting shop in the Uxbridge Road, Madame Sosostris and and I are observing the shapes of clouds and attempting to interpret their significance. She tells me that I will soon go on a long journey by sea (but doesn't know where to) and that I will regret certain things I have done; she tells me to beware of being bitten. This is all too vague; I feel I'm not getting my money's worth. I tell her of my dream last night in which I found spaghetti in my hair. Raw or cooked? Cooked. The strands were sticky with starch and hard to disentangle, so I left them in place. I did exactly the right thing, she tells me, which is gratifying.

CONSTRUCTION SITE

It will be the biggest massage parlour in Europe. There will be conference facilities and underground parking for 500 cars. All rooms will have free internet access, and those for private parties will have jacuzzis and fully stocked bars. Confidentiality will be guaranteed. Training courses will be run offering diplomas in Thai, Japanese, Swedish and Hawaiian massage. The borough council, mindful of the job opportunities it will create and the high-income clients it will attract whose spending power will benefit many other local businesses, has been more than cooperative throughout the planning procedures.

CRANE AT NIGHT

Cranes at night sing in the wind. I have a friend, now in his eighties, who can trace his life's work back to the night when, aged fourteen, he was taken up by his father to the top of a crane to hear the music at its source. Since then he has travelled all over the world making recordings of the cranes' songs. His work has documented the passing of traditional melodies – work songs, lullabies, the sea shanties relayed by the old derricks that used to unload cargoes in seaports – as light-weight new materials came to be used in the construction of cranes.

CRITIC

The critic has decided that a number of handwritten pages, folded and tucked into an ancient children's encyclopaedia bought at a car-boot sale, are part of the first English translation of *Madame Bovary*, made by Juliet Herbert (see page 42) in collaboration with the author himself and brought by her to London in 1857, since when its whereabouts have been unknown. The pages describe not, unfortunately, Emma's seduction by Rodolphe or her trysts with Leon in the hotel room in Rouen, but the visit to the flax mill: 'Nothing could be less curious than this curiosity. A piece of waste ground, on which amid a mass of sand and stones were a few break-wheels, already rusty, surrounded by a quadrangular building pierced by a number of little windows . . .' This is all nonsense, of course, and most scholars say the pages are part of a lazy copy of the Marx Aveling translation with a few words missing, but a critic has got to make his name somehow and at least the paper and ink have been dated by experts to the right period.

CROWD

Near the front of this crowd is a fifteen-year-old boy who gets up early and goes to bed late and who notices things. For example, a large roll of paper tossed onto a skip that turned out to be drawings of a naked girl (see page 82); one of these drawings is now on his bedroom wall, the others he has sold. He runs errands, has good excuses, knows ways and means, scams and fixes, watches who bosses who and takes no side. He blends in. This is an intense and brilliant period of his life. In the next few years he will have to make some tricky decisions, the consequences of which will not always be apparent when he makes them, but the quality of his attention to the world bodes well.

DRIVER WITH POLICE

He has done well for himself, this man, since he came to England in 1971. On the day of his arrival, with no money at all and only the address of his mother's cousin in his pocket, he stood outside Shepherd's Bush Tube station and saw, sitting at a café table, the most beautiful girl in the world. Naturally, on the second day he returned to the same café, where he saw, sitting at the same table, the second most beautiful girl in the world. It was this girl who, three months later, he married, and still loves. Now he owns seven properties, which are rented out, and lives in a large house with enough bedrooms to put up his children and grandchildren when they come to stay; and often when he looks at his wife, he knows that *she* is the most beautiful woman, and the beauty of the first girl was just a trick of the light, or a mirage created by the impressionable mind of a hungry youth on his arrival in the big city. But recently, when he goes to check on his properties or to a meeting with a builder or estate agent, he has been driving slowly, looking at the women walking by on the pavement. Cars behind him sound their horns, while he waits for the women to turn their faces. And now the police have pulled him up for kerb-crawling.

EMPIRE

At the time the Shepherd's Bush Empire was built in 1903, the British Empire comprised around a fifth of the world's land surface area and a quarter of the world's population. This is the kind of heavyweight, exacting matter from which the Empire's music-hall acts provided light relief. Ford Madox Ford, whose work at the office of *The English Review* in Holland Park Avenue was constantly interrupted by visiting authors, used to take the day's submissions to the second-house performance. 'During the duller turns, Ford made his decisions and I duly recorded them,' recalled his assistant. 'But when someone really worth listening to – the late Victoria Monks for example, or Little Tich or Vesta Victoria – appeared on the stage, the cares of editorship were for the moment laid aside.'

ESTATE AGENT'S WINDOW

If I worked in the City and was hugely rich I might just be able to afford a tiny one-bedroom flat, in which I could install my mistress. I would visit her in the afternoons; and then in the evening, in a house that is crowded with children and pets and lists of things to be bought or repaired or otherwise attended to, when my wife asked me about my day, I would tell her about my meeting with a client from Denmark, and her urgent and unexpected demands, which I will hope I have been able to satisfy, and she will look at me with shining eyes.

EXCURSION

We are fourteen years old and have been dragged out of our beds by our enlightened parents who, wanting to show us there is a world beyond W12, are insisting we join a guided literary tour of a neighbouring district, W6. Here is the house where Anthony Burgess lived with his first wife, who died of cirrhosis of the liver: 'To the house in Hammersmith they had had one dozen bottles of Gordon's delivered weekly,' the guide quotes from *Beard's Roman Women*. Here in St Peter's Square (above) is where Robert Graves lived in the 1920s in a *ménage à quatre*, where his lover Laura Riding jumped from a third-floor window (and broke her back) and Graves, in sympathy, jumped from a lower window (and twisted his ankle). Here is the location where B. S. Johnson's Christie Malry determined to get his own back on a cruel, unfeeling world, graduating from stealing office stationery to killing 20,000 people by poisoning their drinking water. Now we are beginning to *like* W6 and to see the appeal of the literary life, but our parents decide that's enough culture for one day and take us home.

FAIRGROUND

In the 1820s, when the middle classes were moving outwards from central London, a regular fair on Brook Green was banned – too much drunkenness and debauchery. Fairs are now more orderly occasions involving roundabouts, dodgems, stalls where you win fluffy dogs for hooking floating ducks, and long queues for the candyfloss, all hemmed in by health-and-safety regulations. But as the afternoon wears on one or both of the Terrible Twins still sometimes makes an unscheduled appearance.

FUNERAL

The old woman who swallowed a fly (see page 108) didn't live for ever, of course. But she'd have been pleased by the turn-out at the funeral: children, grandchildren, one or two babes in arms, sisters and cousins down from the North, besides her local friends she bumped into at the shops, in the market, with whom she chatted about the weather, ailments, the new young doctor. Back in the pub after the service, it is these other old women – although seated, and some in wheelchairs – who dominate. When they want something, they tug the nearest jacket or skirt. 'Lovely legs,' they say, or 'Does she ken what she looks like from behind?', in voices that carry, that are used to speaking to the half-deaf. Strange, to have survived for so long, but no stranger than many other things. They turn their heads, sometimes, these old women, to check that whoever it was who offered them a lift home is still here, or as if looking for something that appears to be missing, which may in fact be the old men, most of whom have long since departed.

GARDEN STATUE

This nymph, dryad, damsel, player of bit-parts in classical myths, is widely available in stone or fibreglass at garden centres. Often she conforms to a standard model that is not without grace: she is modest (strands of hair or folds of a shawl falling between the legs) and yet posed in a way (that slight twist of the hips) that shows off her every curve. Once a year, on the last night of the Julian calendar, she wakes, stretches up her arms, yawns, and looks around her at the punctured football, the rusting barbecue, the plastic children's toys, curious but not surprised.

GEYSER

We live on a thin crust. Underneath, a boiling and bubbling, a witches' brew. The 1937 film of *King Solomon's Mines*★ (starring Paul Robeson as Umbopa) climaxed with a spectacular volcano eruption – apocalyptic doom, a sure-fire crowd-puller – that was staged in the Gaumont studios in Lime Grove, W12 (see page 61); the makeshift special effects may now make the scene appear unrealistic, but not untrue.

★ The novel was written by Rider Haggard while living in W14 in Gunterstone Road; John Gawsworth (page 45) was born in the same road.

GNOMES (3 FOR 2)

It's raining, I'm hungover, I've just got a parking ticket and I live in a world that produces a surplus of garden gnomes but cannot manage to house and feed its most vulnerable inhabitants. Their ruddy cheeks, their dopey assumption of bogus folkloric wisdom . . . Fortunately there are shovels available in the next aisle, for smashing them to bits.

GRAVESTONES

Once upon a time there was a boy with a drum. Once upon a time there was a beautiful princess. Once upon a time there was an old woman who lived alone at the top of a house. Once upon a time there was a man who was always angry, and another who never stopped laughing, and another who killed someone by mistake (although some people said it wasn't a mistake), and a girl who went out to buy a pint of milk, and a pair of twins who were identical except for one thing, and a boy who could pick locks, and a woman who had seven husbands and loved them all, and a man who couldn't make up his mind, and their names are here. Once upon a time there was a man who went on a long journey.

THE GREEN AT 4 A.M.

Shepherd's Bush Green, a traffic-polluted triangle of roughly eight acres of patchy grass with a small children's playground and an area for dogs with signs telling their owners to clean up after them, was once used by shepherds to rest their flocks on the way to Smithfield Market. Late in the nineteenth century the metropolitan board of works purchased the land for under the market rate, because of its unlucky reputation: when shepherds counted their sheep after they had grazed overnight, always two or three were found to be missing, and sometimes lambs were born with malformations. The Green remains a kind of Bermuda Triangle: at night there are figures slumped on the ground who are far gone, lost to the world, and there is one particular bench on which anyone who sits is never seen again.

HAIR SALON

Jennifer is single again. *Grazia* tells me this, in big yellow letters on its cover. I can't say I'm surprised, or worried for her, or even interested at all (Jennifer who?) for longer than the six minutes I am waiting for my haircut. 'So how would you like it today?' So many styles, options, extras, special offers to choose from: no wonder people keep changing their minds. Ulla is away, her baby is due any day, and I wish her well. The new girl leans close and is lovely and smells sweet and it's not hard to imagine that we could spend the rest of our lives together and have fourteen beautiful children – all that's between us is age, circumstances and a pair of very sharp scissors. Afterwards, I slink away, Samson shorn by Delilah ('and his strength went from him'), avoiding the temptation to glance at my reflection in the window of the newsagent's next door. It's all done with mirrors.

HALF-LIVES

After living in W12 for a while, a half-knowledge of some of the faces in the crowd: isn't that the woman from the newsagent's, or the dinner-lady from school? The man from the dry-cleaner's? Outside the locations in which I know them, it's hard to put names to them, but they're teasingly familiar. That's the guy in *EastEnders*, isn't it, the one who's been accused of rape? And there, that's definitely the man who used to call me Raymond, who used to claim I was his best friend and tap me for a tenner to tide him over until the benefits office opened on Monday. In the end I snapped, told him I wasn't Raymond and wasn't going to carry on funding his weekends. Now he's staring straight at me, but without any acknowledgement that he's ever seen me before.

HORSES UNDER THE WESTWAY

Under the Westway flyover, city children learn to ride horses – the open road! the right to roam! – in a tight circle, forever ending up where they began. Just fifty metres from here, marooned between the two-lane slip-roads that join the A40 and almost adjacent to Westfields shopping mall, there is a semi-permanent encampment of so-called Travellers: they pay water rates and council tax, and if they're away for more than a week they lose their right to stay on the site, so they do less travelling than the commuters speeding by (or stuck in a gridlock) above them. I think of Escher's drawings of impossible objects: often multi-storeyed, with stairways and connecting passages that lead both up and down at the same time, immediately familiar to anyone who has worked in a large organisation with all its attendant bureaucracy. The Westway flyover, designed by M. C. Escher.

INCIDENT

Something happened – an *incident*, a police officer tells me, which they are now *forensicating*. A mystery, then. Which makes it appropriate that this little patch should be inviolable, sacrosanct, behind its fluttering tape. The bottles and lager cans lying around suggest that the memories of those involved will be, at the least, a little hazy; eyewitnesses will be hard to trace, and most won't have paid attention until after the event; the forensic evidence (blood, hair, dust) will be inconclusive. Eventually – after a trial, an appeal, a retrial? – an account will be put together, claiming to be definitive. I step into the road, skirting the tape. The sky is bright blue. Outside the Tube station I am offered a free newspaper. Something happened.

INFANTILISM

After his death in 1966 Walt Disney's corpse was cryogenically frozen and is now stored under this garden off the Westway. Exhumed and examined in 1991, the body showed 'evidence of surface fracturing'. The Westway periodically suffers from the same problem; stalled in the traffic queues caused by road repairs, drivers and their passengers attempt to identify these figures, scoring extra points if they can remember the names of all seven dwarfs.

INGERSOLL ROAD

Juliet Herbert, the daughter of a London builder, went to France in the 1850s as the governess of a young girl and became a close friend of the girl's uncle, who was Gustave Flaubert. Juliet and Flaubert together translated *Madame Bovary* into English. She brought the translation back to London, presumably to find a publisher, and no one knows what happened to it. (The first published translation was by Eleanor Marx Aveling, Karl Marx's daughter.) She and Flaubert wrote to each other for twenty years; her letters to him are assumed to have been on the bonfire of private papers he made shortly before he died, his to her have never been found. He visited her in London three times, and she visited him in France. She died in 1909, of 'disease of Heart, duration unknown', at 27 Ingersoll Road, the house shown here.

JOGGER

'Let us go then, you and I ... through certain half-deserted streets ...'
From J. Alfred Prufrock's home to Ravenscourt Park, twice round
the perimeter and back, is two and a half miles. The circumference
of the world is approximately 25,000 miles – which means that after
twenty-seven years and five months he will be able to claim he has
run round the world. He is fifty-three years old ('With a bald spot in
the middle of my hair'), he isn't training for a marathon, he doesn't
have a new lover – so the point of all this isn't obvious. But there is,
nevertheless, a point, and it has something to do with precision, with
the measuring out of life in coffee spoons.

JUNK SHOP

The Last Place on Earth is of course exactly where you do expect to find a collection of plastic dolls, a chamber pot, a 1950s polka-dot summer dress. And a small canoe-shaped (but with open ends) vessel on short legs, inscribed with writing in French, which the shop-keeper confidently declares is a quill rest. The pull of these shops is the ghost that barely adheres, the bygone associations and value – even if very little – attached to these objects by their previous owners: the heirloom kept on a shelf, the dress worn twice and never again, the substance of thought in the pauses when the writer rested the quill on its rest before inking another sentence. (That's my own bike, by the way, pointlessly chained to a very short bollard in front of the shop: lift the chain over and you're away, and another mundane object finds its way into a whole new pattern of meaning. Godspeed.)

KING

The King of Redonda? The title is disputed. The fantasy writer M. P. Shiel claimed in 1929 that his father had assumed sovereignty of Redonda, a tiny uninhabited island in the Caribbean, in 1865 with the approval of Queen Victoria; after his father's abdication, Shiel himself was crowned king in 1880 by the Bishop of Antigua. Or perhaps by Hugh Semper, a peripatetic Methodist minister and family friend. Shiel passed on the title to the writer John Gawsworth (King Juan I), who, bankrupt and suffering from alcoholism, seems to have sold on the title several times before his death in 1970. (Shiel's ashes, kept in a tea caddy by Gawsworth in his West London flat, were occasionally used, according to Barry Humphries, to flavour stews.) Prominent among current pretenders to the throne is the Spanish writer Javier Marías (King Xavier; see his *Dark Back of Time*), who claims to have acquired the title when he bought a collection of Gawsworth's papers at Sotheby's in 1995. Marías has conferred dukedoms on, among others, Almodóvar, Coetzee and Alice Munro.

KITE IN A TREE

A moment ago the kite was soaring, emblem of freedom and pure play; now it's stuck in the branches; but to the child, far more startling than this is her view of her father, who never in a million years will be able to climb that tree. He too has come down to earth – his arms akimbo, his chubby legs spread apart, staring upwards, useless when it counts. Decades of negotiation, of coming to terms, will follow.

KNOCK KNOCK

Who's there? The woman, perhaps, whose father may or may not be dying of liver cancer in Exeter (see page 1). Or someone collecting money for the blind, or someone who will hand you a rainbow-coloured leaflet explaining how all nations upon earth may walk in the path of peace and joy. Just possibly, an unknown lanky teenager who will address you as 'Dad'. Or the Angel Gabriel ('The Holy Spirit shall come on you, and the power of the Highest shall over-shadow you'); and if not him, the other one, Azrael, the Angel of Death, who has your name on a list. Not now, you say, I'm busy. Shall he call back later? Yes, later, some other time.

KNOLL

According to Professor Jeremy Dyson (*Journal of Archaeological Studies*, lxxxiv, 21–8), this knoll or hummock is the burial mound of a royal sovereign and dates from the Period of the Three Kings, during which trade routes were established with settlements on the Gower Peninsula. This didn't put off the tomb-robbers in the late eighteenth century, and nor does it deter the developer who wants to build a suite of executive homes on this plot of land, overgrown with spiky bushes, between the back gardens of two rows of houses. His plans are opposed by many local residents, and by the foxes who have been living here for some years and who have unilaterally declared it the Independent Republic of Foxes. Most people are well disposed towards the foxes, but their random acts of sabotage – which include gnawing through the electric cables that power garden lights – are not attracting much sympathy to their cause.

LAUNDRY

The tradesman's entrance, the back exit. Toad of Toad Hall disguised himself as a washerwoman to escape from prison; Mary Queen of Scots used the same disguise in her attempted escape from Lochleven Castle. In the late 1990s a certain South American ex-dictator visited London to meet up with his old political cronies, many of whom were living here in exile; he stayed incognito in a hotel in W12, but a local journalist recognised him, and when the hotel lobby was invaded by news reporters he sought to escape in a crate of laundry. Discovered when the laundry van was being unloaded, he declared that his conscience was clear, clean as a whistle, white as driven snow.

LIBRARY

Cem learns from the local paper that the author of the Hungarian book in his drawer (see page 11) is giving a talk at the library. He goes along, taking the book with him, thinking that the vanished owner of the book might also be attending, but arrives late and the room is empty. A librarian tells him that the event ended almost as soon as it had begun when a member of the audience claimed he had been insulted by the author and challenged him to a duel, which will take place at dawn the next day on the Green. A misunderstanding, Cem suggests, but she insists this is what happened and adds that the police have been informed. Cem thinks that he himself has perhaps insulted the vanished owner of the book, which is why the man never returned to the café; and he has insulted the author too, whose book he kept in a drawer with the tea towels, and he is lucky to be alive; and the librarian, he can't help noticing, has legs he turns to look at again as he leaves. Several hours later he wakes from a dream flavoured by a mingling of fear, elation and intimacy, and he understands what it must feel like to be a soldier on the night before a battle.

LIT WINDOWS

'On black winter nights he had seen the sparse lights glimmering through the rain and drawing close together, as the dreary road vanished in long perspective. Perhaps this was its most appropriate moment, when nothing of its smug villas and skeleton shops remained but the bright patches of their windows . . .' Lucian, in Arthur Machen's autobiographical *The Hill of Dreams* (written 1895–7), comes from rural Wales to London to write. Living in a room 'between Shepherd's Bush and Acton Vale' off bread, green tea and a black tobacco 'which seemed to him a more potent mother of thought than any drug from the scented East', he experiences the classic *fin-de-siècle* urban alienation: 'One might have sworn that not a man saw his neighbour who met him or jostled him, that here every one was a phantom for the other, though the lines of their paths crossed and recrossed, and their eyes stared like the eyes of live men.' He is found dead at his desk, bent over piles of paper 'covered with illegible hopeless scribblings'. Machen himself became a successful writer, admired by Eliot, Yeats and Borges among others, and lived into his eighties.★

★ A biography of Machen was written by John Gawsworth (see page 45) in the 1930s but not published until 2005.

LOOSE BRICKS IN A WALL

From India to the Balkans there are many legends and ballads telling of women who were walled up alive – troublesome wives, or virgins immured in the foundations of a new building to bring good fortune. In England too, in the guidebooks to medieval castles you can find similar stories. Here, someone has taken pity on the woman and set her free; the bricks hurriedly piled into the opening in the wall will not fool anyone for long, but may give the woman and her rescuer a precious few hours' start.

LOVERS' LANE

Even in densely populated areas there are still lanes, car parks, stretches of waste ground where lovers in cars can meet in the afternoon to talk, have sex or simply stare at the future through a misted-up windscreen. Less often, such isolated spots are favoured by suicides. Anna told me recently of a friend who, after she had quarrelled with her lover and he had driven back to work, discovered she had a flat tyre. Needing help, she approached the single other car in the lane. She knocked on the window, first gently and then (it was raining) with increasing desperation. The door opened, releasing fumes from a tube attached to the car's exhaust pipe and a smell of whisky. The man, woozy but still conscious, eventually staggered out and helped to change her wheel. At that moment, if he had asked to marry her, she'd have let her lover go hang and said yes. She was tempted to ask him herself, but he had a thing he needed to do and she had already interrupted him.

MAN IN A TREE

This man has never learned to swim. On the other hand, he has no fear of heights, because once, when he was about eight or nine years old, he was climbing a tree in a park in Scotland and fell from a good height, and flew. Not far, but instead of plummeting straight down he glided to one side and landed safely about twenty yards from the tree. His father and his older brother witnessed this. It's not a skill he shows off but he knows that if ever he slipped or lost his balance again, he has this ability.

MAN WITH A CAN OF CIDER

I have lived in the same house for eighteen years, and there's rarely been a day I haven't seen this man leaning against the wall outside the Irish pub at the end of the road. He sleeps in a hostel for the homeless, although more than many people who live here (who arrive, breed, completely refurbish their houses and then move on) he could claim this street as his home. If he has any stories, he's not interested in telling them. He talks to me about football, relentlessly. Last week QPR lost 5–1 to Celtic in a pre-season friendly. This weekend they're playing Wycombe Wanderers and should do better. He is the most cheerful and optimistic person I know.

MARKET

Bargains. 'For you, special price.' At a time when expenses budgets were tight, Lawrence Durrell, writer of the exotic, of the Mediterranean and North Africa, of 'the moods of the great verb Love', once posed for a magazine photographer on a chair in Shepherd's Bush market. (His agent lived in W12; Durrell happened also to be a friend of John Gawsworth and a duke of Redonda: see page 45.) The nature/nurture debate, whether heredity or environment determines who we are, is beside the point; it's more about negotiating a good deal with both, about learning how to haggle with the means we have.

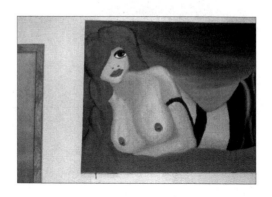

MASSAGE PARLOUR

Extras? You mean, as in 'other services offered'? She runs through a menu of the day's specials and when they say the prices seem a bit expensive she says so is philosophy, which is what she is studying, and it's especially expensive for foreign students and why do they think she's working here, for the fun of it? Some of them ask her what's wrong with a bit of fun, missing the point completely. Some of them make a joke of it, asking how much for the meaning of life. (A *lot*, she says; more than you can afford, little man.) Some of them suggest she should be studying economics, or at least taking a joint degree, and point out that if she charged less she might get more takers. They have a point, she admits; but she is proud of her philosophy essays and her tutor says she has a natural gift and she knows what she's worth.

MEAT

What we require of most animals is their death. It's possible that future generations will look back on our meat-eating habits as barbaric, in the way we now regard stoning people for adultery or institutional racism. In the meantime, rather than vacuum-packed chicken nuggets delivered to the back door of Tesco, I'd far rather see these refrigerated vans parking openly along the Uxbridge Road and the butcher boys strolling nonchalantly along the pavement with a couple of carcasses slung over their shoulder. What you see is what you get.

MILK BOTTLES

How many city children have seen a cow? How many city children have seen a *milk bottle*? I'm lucky to still have them. Their genre is not fast-paced thriller (no quick getaway on a milk cart) or interior psycho-drama (alcohol, not milk, for that), more Ealing comedy★ – local, domestic, jokes based on misunderstandings and inhibitions and the husband being cuckolded by the milkman. Three days a week the clink of the empties being gathered in the milkman's fingers announces the arrival of their replacements; and I step out to collect them from not a gentler but a simpler age, when containers didn't even need labels to tell you what's inside them.

★ The Ealing Comedies were made just a few miles away at the Ealing Studios in W5.

MINICAB OFFICE

I need to get to Heathrow but there's a Tube strike and traffic on the M4 is at a standstill. 'No problem,' the driver says, but there are several: mechanical ones, language ones, and others relating to our different understanding of time, distance and the local topography. He is tall and very thin and softly spoken; he teaches me the Somali words for left and right, or perhaps north and south, and, when we are stopped at a red light, a word that clearly applies to attractive women. I jab at the face of my watch, which he compares with his own and smiles: it is not broken. We zigzag through Hounslow, Feltham, Stanwell. In the late afternoon, after taking a wrong turning on the Heathrow perimeter road, we have a puncture beside the reservoir at Staines. Searching for the spare wheel, the driver emerges instead with a fishing rod. Rush-hour traffic stops and starts around us; planes fly low overhead. As we sit for a while in silence, smoking, gazelle and hartebeest come down to the water to drink.

NEW HOUSING

Gaumont Terrace, Gainsborough Court: clean lines, sparkling windows, flowers blooming – estate-agent brochure material. In the night, a bird alights on a lamp-post and preens; a heavy-set man shuffles across the road carrying a large double-bass case; a sudden scream, then silence. Alfred Hitchcock worked on this site when it was occupied by film studios: built in 1914 by Gaumont, converted to sound in 1927, rebuilt in 1932–3, used by Gainsborough Pictures in the 1940s to make propaganda films and historical romances. Bought by the BBC in 1949, it was a warren of studios, store rooms, corridors, staircases, rickety fire escapes and locked doors; when they made *Steptoe and Son* in the 1960s, the bleak comedy about a Shepherd's Bush rag-and-bone merchant, it was said they didn't need to build a set.

NEW KEYS

Emma, the woman who took delivery of a packing crate (page 67), is having a set of keys copied for her new boyfriend. She's had new locks put in, because the boyfriend she broke up with never gave his own keys back. He's still in the area, just a few streets away, and Emma has been seeing him around so frequently that she's come to believe this can't be accidental, that he must be stalking her. The last time she saw him she went up to him and told him this. No, he said, it was *she* who was stalking *him*: he couldn't get her out of his mind, she wouldn't leave him alone.

NO BALL GAMES

I used to think that signs like these were clues (some of them ana-grams: MANGO LABELS) in a kind of treasure hunt, and that if I solved them all, and in the right order, then I'd win a prize. Now I realise that they are put in place by a hidden brotherhood of priests desperate to resist a rising tide of blasphemy and impurity; that they all mean essentially the same thing ('Please do not touch'); and that to remain human and free we must play ball games wherever and whenever we want.

NOT HERE

87 per cent of the time I'm anywhere but here – I'm tired or pre-occupied or have my nose stuck in a book, and sometimes even then I'm not attending to the words but to a fly crawling slowly across the page. Often I neither hear what's being said to me ('I'm sorry, forgive me, I was somewhere else') nor see what's in front of me. I once sat for ten minutes in a car staying resolutely calm in front of a sign I read as DO NOT PANIC HERE, until I glanced in the wing mirror and saw a traffic warden approaching.

OFFICE BUILDING

The BBC building at White City occupies the site of the stadium for the 1908 Olympics. There were the usual scandals, cock-ups and bruised egos: in the marathon, the leading runner collapsed on entering the stadium, was helped across the finishing line and then disqualified; in the men's 400 metres, all except one of the athletes refused to take part in a re-run of the final, leaving a single contender to run – or jog – around the track before collecting his gold medal. Sport now takes up even more airtime than it did then, and with good reason: even those contemptuous of competition and celebrity must be drawn in by the mixed emotions of those who come second, who so very nearly get (but don't) what they desire and feel they deserve.

ON CAMERA

They can't get enough of us. On the streets, in the car parks, in shops and malls and every public space we are filmed, recorded, analysed. The eye of God, voyeurism of the banal. And lest we think that they are concerned only with the pattern of our movements, that they don't value us as individuals, sometimes they hold a microphone in front of our face and ask for our personal opinions on everything from detergents to the latest shock-horror news. Best to keep this bland and predictable – if they really knew what we think, the whole system would judder to a halt. 'It's disgusting – she should resign.' 'They were a lovely couple, always smartly dressed, kept themselves to themselves.'

PAVEMENT WITH CHALK RECTANGLE

One morning a few months ago a packing crate was delivered to the house of the woman, Emma, who lives here. About five feet long by two feet wide by three feet high, it could have contained a library of pornographic videos, or two folded illegal immigrants, or everything she had ever lost. Apart from hers, the only address on the crate was that of a transport company in Tallinn, Estonia. The van driver and his mate unloaded the crate onto the pavement but said they were not obliged to carry it up the steps into the house. Emma waited for her boyfriend to come home. At lunchtime the crate was still there, but when she looked out of the window at five o'clock it had gone. She never told her boyfriend about the crate, and shortly afterwards they broke up.

PICK-UP

I'm stopped at a traffic lights in pouring rain, waiting to turn left. Someone knocks on the passenger-side window, and when I wind it down there's a girl asking for a lift. Where to? Hammersmith. It's where I'm going. She gets in beside me and slumps down in the seat, the rain dripping off her jacket, her skirt riding up her thighs. 'It's not far,' I tell her, 'you could take a bus.' She looks about eighteen but is maybe younger. She asks if I can spare a tenner. I tell her no, and besides, even if I could, she'd only spend it on drugs. She agrees. But just a tenner, surely I must have that in my wallet? I ask her why I should give it her, what's in it for me. She looks at me directly and laughs. 'Anything,' she says, 'anything you want.' Now it has stopped raining and King Street looks washed and shiny in the sunshine, and I'm thinking (along with what *do* I want?) of how everything happens at so many levels at once, levels that slide across each other and only occasionally intersect, when suddenly she slaps my knee and I jam on the brakes, just in time to miss an old man who is shuffling across the street with his shopping trolley. She shakes her head. Close, she says.

PIGEONS

During the siege of the Shepherd's Bush Commune in 1870, carrier pigeons were used to bring in messages from the Commune's allies. The pigeons were sent out in baskets attached to balloons, and returned with messages wrapped in goose quills attached to their tail feathers. The system was far from foolproof: some of the pigeons were killed by hawks or guns, and others were captured by the enemy and returned with false information. But pigeons are still treated here with respect and affection. (Underground as well as overground communication networks are also recorded: behind the corrugated iron in the above photograph is the entrance to a tunnel, one of several extending into neighbouring boroughs. Most were originally built by smugglers, but at times when the borders of W12 were more strictly controlled they were also used by refugees wishing to escape to what they believed were more liberal territories; sometimes these refugees met others – from SW3, say, or even south of the river – travelling in the opposite direction.)

PIRATES

Pirates (I mean pirates of the kind that have only one leg and a parrot perched on their shoulder) were invented in W12. Long John Silver in *Treasure Island* was based by Stevenson on the poet W. E. Henley – who lived in Shepherd's Bush, who had a leg amputated when he was a child, and who was described by Stevenson's stepson as 'a great, glowing, massive-shouldered fellow with a big red beard and a crutch; jovial, astoundingly clever, and with a laugh that rolled like music; he had an unimaginable fire and vitality'. Henley appealed to Stevenson in the way that pirates fascinate children, and childhood was something Stevenson approved of: 'I am sure that playthings are the very pick of life . . . I shall conform for a little to the ways of [the] foolish world; but so soon as I have made enough money, I shall retire and shut myself up among my playthings until the day I die.' In books, he wrote in a letter to Henley, 'I want to hear swords clash.' After writing several plays together the two men eventually quarrelled (over matters of literary style). But Stevenson's instinct was right: literature *needs* pirates. 'When Henley and his gang of pirates came upon the scene,' Ford Madox Ford recalled, 'it meant that some sort of interest was taken in the literary world.'

POLITICS

There was period when Michael – young, good-looking, with a job in the planning department of the local council – seemed to be expected to have answers to more questions than he had even thought about. What were his views on euthanasia, abortion, animal rights, the national debt? All this recycling business, it's just another way of raising money, isn't it? As he emerged from the town hall for his lunch break, complete strangers came up to shake his hand and wish him good luck; others accused him of fiddling his expenses. Anxious parents sought his help in getting their children into schools or out of prison. And then one evening it clicked: his girlfriend, leafing through the junk mail, picked out a flyer from one of the candidates for the forthcoming general election and told him to look at the photograph. He shook his head, but she insisted: the resemblance was uncanny. The next day he didn't shave, and wore a T-shirt and jeans to work instead of his usual suit and tie. He's still ambitious, still knows what he wants from life, but he takes care now not to appear too confident of achieving it.

PROBATIONARY DRIVER

In the months after Ted's wife died the various ailments that had kept him virtually housebound began to clear up. Perhaps, the new young doctor suggested, they had all been simply allergic reactions – to the fabric of his wife's clothes or the perfume she favoured, something habitual about her. He began to go out more. He taught himself to cook. At the age of seventy-three, he took driving lessons. Prepare, observe, manoeuvre; engage clutch, check mirror, move off. You don't need super-intelligence; and like table manners or the steps of a dance, this is a routine that, once mastered, becomes automatic. But he found it difficult, not least because he was well aware that what stopped it coming easily was the amount of effort he was putting into it. At his third attempt, he passed the test. Now he drives most days along certain regular circuits. But he has bought P-plates, to tell other drivers to treat him gently; and he still lacks confidence in making right-hand turns, which involve crossing an opposing stream of traffic, so has to plan his route carefully to make sure he only has to turn left.

RAILINGS

Take a stick and trail it along the railings. Change the angle, the speed, the pressure – compose your own soundtrack as you go. And do it now, while the mood's upon you. The railings go on and on (keeping things in, keeping things out), but not the child's unselfconscious glee in the noise to be made from them.

RECYCLING

Waste not, want not: an imperative during wartime rationing, which went on long after the war itself had ended. At the top of a certain hill my mother would switch off the car's engine and we'd coast down in an eerie silence: look, no petrol! Sheets were turned sides to middle, with the ridge of the seam down the centre of the bed, forcing me to choose one side or the other. Bars of carbolic soap, hundreds of them, were stored in the garage; this now strikes me as sinister. Here we are again, but this time making a virtue of superfluity, bringing offerings to these back-door altars of the gods of consumerism. Waste is sin, and everything past its use-by date shall be changed into something new. Or if not changed, then become part of the global village: scrap iron from Kerala turns up in bijou shops in Covent Garden, the bobble hats of Queens Park Rangers supporters now adorn the heads of refugees in Africa.

SANITARY WARE

All public toilets and washbasins in W 12 are designed by contemporary artists. This enlightened policy dates back to the 1920s, when US Customs ruled that a sculpture by Constantin Brancusi was subject to a 40 per cent sales tax as manufactured metal in the category 'Kitchen Utensils and Hospital Supplies'. Brancusi appealed; witnesses praised the work's 'harmonious proportions' and 'beautiful sense of workmanship', and the court found in his favour, declaring the work 'pleasing to look at and highly ornamental'. (Hovering in the wings was Marcel Duchamp, who had travelled to New York with the crates of Brancusi's sculptures and who had first exhibited his urinal, titled *Fountain*, ten years before; he's still hovering when, caught short on my way home from the pub, I place my coin in the slot and visit this facility on the Green.)

SCANDAL

Shame. Fame. The author's publisher commented: 'We are not in a position to confirm or deny the content of this story, and we do not generally comment on the private lives of individual authors. However, we expect everyone associated with this company to demonstrate high levels of personal and professional integrity and we take all allegations of inappropriate behaviour seriously. That said, we are pleased to announce that the final part of the author's new translation of the *Confessions* of St Augustine has been delivered, and we are bringing forward publication to the earliest possible date.'

SCHEDULE

Assembled at the meeting point, these newly arrived foreign students will be given maps, directions, timetables, contact numbers. Most will stick to the schedule; one or two will stray, go walkabout, become lost – which is the best thing they can do, being the whole point of travel. (In stories, when someone gets lost you know something interesting or even magical is going to happen.) Getting lost at home, in a district choked with habit and familiarity, is harder (this is where drugs come in), but happily there are still times when I feel I hardly know this place, I've only a slim idea of where I am.

SCHOOL

If a man and his wife can mow a field in two days and they get paid £3.50 a field and their rent is £40 pounds a month and beer costs 10p a pint and they each drink five pints a night (it's thirsty work) and on the seventh day the wife discovers her husband is having an affair with the neighbour's daughter and throws him out and her two children help with the mowing but they can work at only a third of the pace of the husband and on the tenth day the rent goes up by 10 per cent and on the eighteenth day the wife gets ill, what is the difference at the end of the month between the rent they owe and what they can pay? Assume all fields are level.

SHOP FRONT

In the back of this shop there is a room where men play cards and smoke. The light is low; they know one another's faces well enough. Usually they play for small sums of money; sometimes, in the small hours, the stakes are high: cars, property, the clothes they stand up in. If I say that there are men in this back room who have staked the title deeds to land in the Old Country that was nationalised but which may now be reclaimed, the room is imbued with history and nostalgia; if I say that there are men who have staked their daughters, the nostalgia curdles.

SINGLE SHOES

So many single shoes – lying in the middle of the road, in the gutter, on the pavement (another one is on page 83). Yet I have never seen anyone walking around with just their remaining shoe. Where have they gone, these people? What canyon of passion or despair have they leapt, never to be seen again? We walk around them, our minds filled with shopping lists; by the end of the week they'll have gone, removed by the street-cleaners; they speak of abandon.

SKELETON OF BICYCLE

This is a tedious urban cliché, empty of all meaning. By tomorrow morning the saddle, handlebar, chain and pedals will have gone the way of the wheels but the lock will still be there, and that's it. Of more interest is the railing, which is a replica of one of a series installed during the First World War at locations in W12 chosen personally by Councillor Joseph Chadback. While upholding the right of the Suffragettes to make their political protests, Chadback was determined that their habit of chaining themselves to railings should not disrupt the free flow of traffic and pedestrians.

SKIP

The white roll in this skip is not posters for a film that's no longer showing or rejected samples from an advertising agency but drawings of a Macedonian girl who speaks almost no English but has a body to die for. The drawings were made by the American artist W. K. Teevald; during his month-long stay in London, where he'd come to supervise the hanging of a retrospective exhibition of his work, he checked out of his hotel and moved in with this girl, and he considers the drawings to be the best work he's done for years. On the day of his return flight to Los Angeles the taxi he'd ordered didn't arrive, so he loaded his bags into the only car available from the nearest mini-cab office. The drawings were strapped onto the roofrack. 'No problem, mister, the Lord is good, he will take best care,' said the driver as he yanked on the rope and knotted it. He looked about twelve years old and was grinning; he could have been making a joke, except that the Virgin Mary was stickered all over the dashboard and a crucifix dangled from the rear-view mirror. When they arrived at the airport the roofrack was bare: not even a shred of rope was clinging to the metal frame. The driver demanded twice the fare that had been agreed before they'd set out and followed Teevald into the departures hall, pleading for justice and if not justice then charity, until he was turned away by security guards.

SLIPPERY PAVEMENT

'The difference between man's vocation and woman's seems naturally to be this . . . He has to go and seek out his path; hers usually lies close under her feet' (Dinah Craik, *A Woman's Thoughts about Women*, 1858). But sometimes the pavements can be slippery, sometimes both he and she can stumble. In 1847 Charles Dickens, with money from a wealthy patron, set up Urania House in Lime Grove, W12, a home for fallen women in which they were trained in 'order and punctuality, cleanliness, the whole routine of household duties' before being sent out to the colonies as maidservants. Dickens involved himself directly in the day-to-day running of Urania House for twelve years; he interviewed the women, he chose the staff, he oversaw a regimen dedicated to 'the formation of habits of firmness and self-restraint'. Then he became distracted by other matters, including his affair with an eighteen-year-old actress and his separation from his wife.

SMASHED WINDOW

We chat while walking down to the Tube; someone calls across the street to a friend; someone else is mumbling to himself, or perhaps talking on his mobile, it's hard to tell the difference. All these words (in Arabic, Turkish, Polish, Gujarati, as well as English) are absorbed by the street as we pass along. Even the words of the angry man by the bus stop – stamping his feet, waving his arms, screaming 'Fuck *you*! Fuck *you*!' – these words too, once we've checked that he hasn't got a machete in his hand, are absorbed, assimilated. But sometimes the words aren't there, or they are not enough, and a brick gets chucked through a window.

STEPS DOWN

There used to be a Polish restaurant down these steps, more of a club than a restaurant. Anton's father, Pavel, used to come here regularly in the late 1930s and 1940s. Pavel's own father, who fought with the German army in the First World War, ended that war in a POW camp in Feltham and stayed on in England. In the Second World War Pavel fought with the British, and lost an arm at Monte Cassino. After 1945 most of the habitués of this club opted to remain in England, but Pavel obstinately, perversely, set off for Poland. One night before the war, aged only seventeen, Pavel had recklessly intervened when he saw two women being assaulted on the river bank in Chiswick. The women were sisters, White Russian émigrés. One of them told fortunes with playing cards, and on the night when Pavel fought off her assailants she took him back to her house, bandaged a knife wound in his arm, laid out her cards and told Pavel that he would one day return to his father's native land and live to a very old age. After reaching Poland Pavel, unable to work because of his war injury, lived for the rest of his life in a square, grey, unlovely block of apartments in a village near the East German border with his wife and their son, Anton, who could not wait to leave.

S.U.V.

He works in television, she runs some kind of agency for artists. As well as this SUV, they have three children, a dog, a nanny, a burglar alarm, a place in the West Country for weekends . . . The registration letters of this vehicle are JEA – which may be his initials, or may have no significance at all, or may stand for *Je est un autre*: the words of Rimbaud, the hallucinating French genius who stopped writing poetry in his twenties and became a gun-runner in Abyssinia, where his letters were filled with complaints about the rain, packages he had not received and money he was owed.

TELECOMMUNICATIONS

Trouble coming: from the way they walk as a couple and yet apart, he can see even before they reach the counter that the woman and the man with her cannot bear each other. The woman's phone is broken and she says it's insured but it isn't, but it's the same number she says, her anger beginning to bite, but a different phone he says and then the man joins in and they are angry together, determined and righteous, for once in a blue moon finding common cause, and eventually he agrees to phone head office. While he is on the phone and they are checking the files, the dates, the numbers, the models, the woman and her partner sit down and he sees the man's hand on her knee and then she turns to him and they kiss, lovingly, and he feels used, used and taken for granted, like a piece of convenient technology.

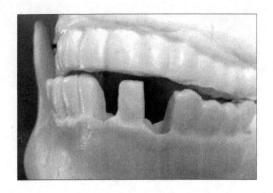

TOOTHACHE

On Friday night Keith felt a shooting pain immediately below his lower front teeth, just to the right. He took some paracetamol but woke in agony in the early hours and couldn't get back to sleep. He had two days to get through, he calculated, until Monday morning, when either his dentist would cure the pain or (far more likely) it would mysteriously disappear the moment he entered the dentist's surgery. During Saturday he nursed his toothache with garlic and clove oil mixed with pepper while attempting to work on his history of the French Revolution in rhyming couplets; but the rhymes wouldn't come, refusing to jump the barrier of pain in his gum. Even a sonnet on dejection, inspired by his feeling of being separated from the world by a veil of misery, didn't get past the first line. The guillotine, he thought – at least it would be quick. And more reliable than a drunken oaf with a blunt axe. On Sunday he phoned a friend and they met up with a group of other neo-formalist poets in a pub. Alcohol offered some relief, but there happened to be some free-verse poets also in the pub and their debate, fuelled by several hours of drinking, became increasingly heated. Just before closing time a fight broke out; Keith was punched in the face and lost his two front teeth.

TRAFFIC JAM

There are days when the sky hangs low and the force of gravity becomes stronger. Cars are fused to the roads. People walk with an effortful slowness through viscous, resistant air; they are retarded, bovine; there's no spark of recognition between them, their speech is slurred and they fumble deep and long in their pockets for the coins they need to buy their newspapers outside the Tube station. Once, I was stuck in a traffic jam when a car travelling at speed on the other side veered towards me, and the couple of seconds before impact were played out in slow motion – I had time to notice the silver stud in the earlobe of the driver, and the pendant swinging above the dashboard, a charm to avert the Evil Eye. On that day, the other car swerved aside at the final instant, clipping my wing mirror. On these slow days, seconds expand to a lifetime, and there is no last-minute escape.

TRAFFIC WARDEN

Hug a traffic warden. He too has children to feed and bills to pay, and each morning he ventures out into a world that is predisposed to treat him as scum. Right now he is writing out a ticket for David's car (see page 6). The only inhuman and therefore incorruptible thing about him is his bulky pack of technology into which he keys your car's registration number – which links to the DVLA, your credit card and bank accounts, your entire recorded history, so that if he doesn't meet your eyes it's because he knows where you were on Friday and the porn sites you've subscribed to. Once keyed in, the number cannot be deleted.

TRAIN AT PLATFORM 1

Early one morning in the summer of 18–, the train drew in to the station of the small town of S— and a single passenger stepped onto the platform . . . These days not only is the train overcrowded, standing room only, but there are automatic ticket barriers and security staff at the exit and CCTV and no one gets through without a permit, a license, a credit card and an approved reason to be where they are. Even so, the occasional stranger still disembarks – the one bringing radical ideas from abroad, who navigates by different stars, who falls inconveniently in love, whom we depend on to get the whole story in motion.

TROUSERS

Far too long, although the waist was a good fit. Perhaps he was shrinking. In the fitting room of the shop a mouse scurried from its hole in the skirting board and paused to watch him. Who did he think he was? The mouse made a short laughing noise, which could have been a sneeze, and then vanished. Unwilling to have wasted his shopping trip entirely, on his way to return the trousers he picked up a pair of unexceptional socks. He took the socks to the pay counter and handed the woman a ten-pound note. The woman took a plastic bag of pound coins from the till, lifted it to her mouth and tore it open with her teeth – ripped it, with a sudden upward swerve of her head, a movement like that of a tiger yanking flesh from the bone of an antelope. He could see the woman's cleavage, the hollow between her breasts that was dark and warm. The coins spilt from the plastic bag and rattled in the hard drawer of the till.

TWO CHAIRS AND PIGEONS

These chairs are in the back yard of an old people's home I sometimes visit, where there is a ninety-year-old man whose constant ex-
pression is one of surprise. Miracles happen, he seems to be saying.
And there are those – quite apart from the Anglicans around here
(and the Methodists, Baptists, Anabaptists, Pentecostalists, etc) and the
Muslims of various persuasions and the Irish Catholics and the Polish
Catholics and the Greek Orthodox, Rastas, and all the others from
the Aaronites to the Zoroastrians – for whom this is enough. Not
so much speaking in tongues (you walk into Damas Gate and start
speaking in fluent Arabic to the woman behind you in the queue)
or winning the lottery, or that (given the number of bad drivers and
sharp edges in the world) so many children survive into adulthood,
but the existence of life itself. Four billion years and still going, despite the incalculable odds against it.

TWO DOGS

The dog with its ears sticking out has strong right-wing opinions, and no small talk at all. The failing education system, immigration and women priests, corruption and drug-taking in sport – the solutions, in his view, are blindingly obvious, and it's only the stupidity of those in charge that keeps us all in our present mess. The bigger dog gets by on his looks; he likes a romp in the park, a good bone and a comfortable bed, and you won't get much from him in terms of intellectual conversation.

UNDERGROUND

There's a man in the carriage who is meticuously peeling an orange and placing the strips of peel in his jacket pocket. There's also a wearisome drunk, making loud but random attempts at communication. The rest of us avoid eye contact. Briefly he focuses on a woman who, tucked neatly in her seat, is reading a textbook titled *Advanced Audit and Assurance*, but soon admits defeat, managing to bore even himself before he can get a rise out of her. She looks too frail, this woman, to be carrying this heavy book around, too intelligent to be giving over her life to numbers, too young for all of this, and in my unbearably meddling and patronising way – not unlike the tedious drunk in this – I think she should come up for some air and light. But she's tough, and not just studious but determined; she knows where she is going, and station by station – occasionally she glances up, counting them off – she is getting there.

VAN WITHOUT AN ENGINE

It's not the end of the road, quite. The roof of this van is intact, and occasionally some drifter stumbles up the alley, tries the door, finds it unlocked and settles in for the night. While in the van each vagrant dreams a new segment of a single enveloping dream. Many of them leave early, before the owner arrives to throw them out; but in fact the owner rarely visits, so there's no hurry to depart. Some return for another night, wanting to find out what happens next, but the segments of the dream are not consecutive.

VANISHING POINT

Kieran, the youngest son of a wealthy Irish family – the one who never got punished, whose shoulders were never expected to bear burdens – lived in this street in the 1970s in a house that belonged to his parents. He rented out rooms to foreign students, and there were frequent parties, and always people coming and going. He told exaggerated stories about his work and love affairs, and every few months he went back to Ireland for the peace and quiet he needed to work on his novel – which was set at the time of the Great Famine in the 1840s; or was based, with her blessing, on the life of an American film actress. The first six chapters were with an agent; the entire first draft had been lost on a train. In the early 1980s, a few weeks after IRA bombs had exploded in Regent's Park and Hyde Park, killing eight soldiers and seven horses, Kieran's novel was published. *Crossing the Border* was a political thriller set in contemporary Northern Ireland. Kieran went over to Ireland to publicise the book at a literary festival. He was seen leaving his hotel and getting into a waiting taxi, but he never arrived at the festival venue. In London his house was broken into and his diaries and files stolen. The students who had lived in his house and who were traced by the police remembered him fondly: there was something both promising and insubstantial about Kieran, as if he was always about to depart.

VILLAGE HALL

On the evening of 22 October 1921 Hugo Macfarlane addressed a meeting in this hall on the topical subject of free love. (In March of the same year Marie Stopes had founded the first family planning clinic in London.) During the meeting a scuffle broke out at the front of the hall, in which a twenty-two-year-old woman fell from the stage and suffered a spinal injury. Macfarlane went on to found a community in Kent that practised vegetarianism, pacifism and free love. (By this term they meant simply that no loving relationship should be regulated by law; it was only in later decades that free love became synonymous with promiscuity.) At one point the community numbered twenty-seven people, but after four years only three remained. Macfarlane returned to London, where for the rest of his life he lived with and cared for the woman who had been injured in this hall, and who was confined to a wheelchair.

W12, LONDON, ENGLAND

My house, my street, W12, London, England, United Kingdom, Europe,
the Northern Hemisphere, the world, the Solar System, the Milky Way, the
universe . . . This is how you write your address as a child, with all
of space (and time, since day one of the universe around 13.5 billion
years ago) revolving around you. Later, when you realise you're not
at the centre of the whole shebang but a mere dot in an infinite con-
tinuum, the magic of your address lies in its sheer improbability, how
easily it could be otherwise or nowise. Actually you are both central
and irrelevant, the two viewpoints equally true and equally illusory;
so that when England make an early exit from the World Cup after
a 4–1 defeat you can choose between feelings of humiliation and
complete indifference.

WALKING THE DOG

Impossible not to think, as I watch the dog-owners and their dogs plodding glumly around the dog-exercising enclosure in the park, of prisoners tramping around the exercise yard in a prison. And not to wonder, as the owners bend to scoop up their dogs' mess in plastic bags, what crimes they have committed to be made to endure this shame. And then I remember that in all prisons there are prisoners who are there in error, who are entirely innocent, who are the victims of miscarriages of justice.★

★ Such as, very probably, Malcolm Kennedy, who was sentenced to life imprisonment in 1991 for the murder of Patrick Quinn at Hammersmith police station; whose conviction was quashed in 1993; who after two retrials was convicted of manslaughter; who was released on parole in 1996; who in the eyes of many was framed by the police and is an innocent man but who now wishes only 'to put the past behind him'.

WATCHMENDER

My 1930s Longines watch, which used to be my father's, has stopped. There is dust in this shop, and more dead clocks than living ones, but the watchmender's eyes are keen and bright. After I've undone the strap he takes my hand, turns it palm upwards, and feels with his dry, soft fingers for the radial artery in my wrist. A pause, and then there it is, the steady underground beat of my pulse. He smiles. He is telling me, I think, that there's life in the old watch yet and he can get it ticking again, but he can't guarantee for how long.

WEDDING CAKES

Bobo, the younger brother of the man who owns this patisserie, has a thing about weddings. He hangs around churches and the registry office, an uninvited but never unwelcome guest on the happy day. He also makes wedding cakes, ever more elaborate, none less than three tiers high, far more of them than are ever commissioned. Some are given away to a home for old people, who have a sweet tooth. The icing on the cakes displayed in the patisserie window gradually hardens and discolours, while the insides become dry and stale. The miniature figures on the top are frozen in poses of remote heroism, like lost polar explorers. The rising divorce rate doesn't worry Bobo in the least, because most people who separate soon marry again.

WEDDING DRESS

Hands off. Fair enough: this dress will probably be worn on one occasion only. This has nothing to do with girls having to be virgins on their wedding day; it's simply about good manners. And at a time when even in museums everything is supposed to be accessible and interactive – touch! smell! taste! play! – the idea of there being limits, boundaries you respect, has an appeal. If this contradicts the text on page 63, so be it; the last thing I'd claim for this book is consistency.

WHAT THE CAT BROUGHT IN

Cats are not stupid. After Ken broke up with Emma (see page 62), his cat sensed his unhappiness and responded with lavish affection, purring and rubbing against his legs and nestling close on his pillow when he went to bed. And then, while he slept, the cat went hunting, bringing home tributes from the natural world – so that each morning, in the first months of his separation from his belovèd, Ken was greeted when he went into the kitchen by the limp body of a sparrow, a pigeon, a mouse, and had to bend to the floor to remove the corpse and wipe away the clots of fresh blood.

WHITE STONE DOG

For his final resting in peace, the black-eyed white dog has chosen a
spot in the lee of Clifton House – out of the wind, getting the best
of the afternoon sun. Far less lonely than he'd be in a cemetery, he's
detached but still close enough to the swing of things to catch the
gossip outside Al Fakher's Shisha Garden, the whiff of kebabs and
curries. That stretch of shops, most of them eateries, is like the Via
Dolorosa: from east to west, it runs Turkish, Indian, something called
Venus, Lebanese, East African, 'Continental', Caribbean, Polish, and
then a funeral parlour; and then the afterlife, a boarded-up corner
premises with a large TO LET sign. This is consecrated ground.

WOMAN WAITING

One morning in 1911 Edith Connaught waited on the corner of
Wood Lane and the Uxbridge Road to meet her lover, Arthur
Winegrass. Edith was pregnant; Arthur's parents disapproved of her,
and the couple were planning to elope. Arthur was due to arrive at
8 o'clock with the money for their rail tickets. But he didn't come.
Edith bore the child, whom she named Arthur, and went to live
with an aunt in Wales. She married a farm-worker and went with
him to Canada in the early 1920s, leaving the child with her aunt.
A few years later, established with her husband on a farm of their
own, Edith sent money to her aunt to pay for Arthur's passage to
Canada. The aunt saw him off at Cardiff docks, but he never arrived
at the farm. Edith and her husband had three children; the youngest,
Annie, married an Italian she met in Europe during the war and had
a son, who himself married in 1970 and had a daughter, Ellen, who
is the woman in this photograph. Every year for the past eight years
Ellen has travelled from Canada to London and on the morning of
6 September has waited for one hour at the corner of Wood Lane
and the Uxbridge Road.

WRITER'S BLOCK

It's not exactly Les Deux Magots, this café, but there are writers here, doing what they do – stretching out a single espresso for most of the morning while they rewrite the opening chapter and check the cricket scores. How long can the waitress leave him in peace, when there are are other customers needing a table? If the café is to stay in business and she is to keep her job, not long at all. But there's a cultural argument too: writers need time to develop their talent, and no interruptions. She could decide (and publishers have been known to do this) on the basis of how good-looking he is, or famous. Or she could ask to read what he's writing (it could be about her). Or a glass of orange juice might get accidentally spilt over his laptop, which would open things up a bit.

YAWN

There was an old woman who swallowed a fly. She was yawning, and the doomed fly happened to be passing as her mouth closed. Then she swallowed a spider — simple curiosity, to know how it tasted and felt; this was something she hadn't done, as far as she could remember, in her seventy-nine years and time was running out, and there was indeed a tickling and maybe a jiggling as it went down. And then the bird. But not whole, and not raw — she was old, but not gaga. A pigeon, which she cooked with bacon, mushrooms and a little brandy, and some black truffles from a jar that her daughter had brought back from France. A retired vicar with time on his hands and a healthy appetite came over to share this meal, which they ate with prunes on the side, and she stopped there — no cat, dog, cow, horse. Despite or because of her curiosity, she stayed fit and healthy for many years, far longer than had been expected by her children, for whom the sale of the old woman's house would have provided useful money in difficult times.

YOGA ADVERTISEMENT

There was a man named Harry Larkyns who took things literally, and who signed up for a yoga course because the girl in the advertisement was not only beautiful but appeared to be good-natured and friendly, and he wanted to meet her. He attended all the classes; he did the stretches, the bends, the poses, the breathing exercises; he hung around afterwards to check who was coming out of the advanced classes; but after three months, although there were many more women students at the college than men and some of them were beautiful and some of them were friendly, he still hadn't found this perfect girl. He demanded his money back. The college refused, but eventually gave him the name of the advertising agency which had produced the poster. Harry wrote to the agency, asking for the contact details of the girl; in his letter he practised some mild deceit, claiming to be someone he wasn't.

Z

You can get stuck for a while in the one-way system, but sooner or later you arrive at the border of W12 and have to make a decision. You're on your own here, and books aren't much help. Stevenson's *Master of Ballantrae*, when faced with a forking of the ways while lost in the forests of North America, resorted to tossing a coin: "'I know no better way,' said he, "to express my scorn of human reason.'" In Isak Dinesen's 'Echoes', Pellegrina Leoni, who claims she was once an angel and 'can still flutter a little, from one place to another', asks Niccolo 'the question which every day comes back and makes life burdensome' – "'Tell me then,' said she, "whether to go to the right or to the left.'"

INDEX

ⒸⒷ *editions*

www.cbeditions.com